I0530923

The Sun, Sex, Blood and Time

Alejandro Colliard

First edition in Spanish: February 2011

Colliard, Alejandro

The Sun, Sex, Blood and Time. - a ed. - Mar delPlata : el autor, 2014.
E-Book.

ISBN 978-987-33-8000-6

1. Literatura Argentina. 2. Narrativa Erótica. I. Título
CDD A863

Fecha de catalogación: 07/04/2014

Traductor: Maria Luz Insausti

The Sun, Sex, Blood and Time

To Daniel Rojas Pachas

Mar del Plata[1] is not at peace. The density in the air condemns the clouds to cry. The drops on the streets reflect warm neon lights and cover the footsteps of a few pedestrians forced by the circumstances to walk. A piece of paper wants to float, it does the narrow path between the sidewalk and the parked cars, to lose itself in the mystery of a gutter. Meanwhile, traffic congregates and visibility becomes difficult due to a thick water curtain. Everything leads inside, and you might as well find somewhere. It´s a pity rain doesn´t

---

[1] Big town Mar del Plata, with a human landscape that procreates indifference among gestures without expression. Mother who adopts liberally, to raise adrift orphans of a thousand places and her own as well. A city that grows with concrete stamens, facing a barefoot ocean, where the salty breeze carries the pollen from beings, through tar canals and fertilizes a territory of anonymous stories.

7

speak. Loneliness is a killer and, at this moment, bullets are smiles.

The blurry windows of an apartment crowned by the shade hide the scarce clarity of the outside. In one of the bedrooms, the pale flashes from the television bounce on the walls, and hit a young woman sitting on one side of the bed. She manipulates a paper envelope, too small to be a letter or a Congratulations Card. The crystals inside fall slowly on the glass that protects the family pictures on the bedside table. Her nose becomes water, but she does not despair. Like a shaman with a potion or a meticulous chef, she disintegrates the white elixir with a blade, to form a thin line, the limit between her misfortune and whatever the future brings. To the fine ready powder she bows and, with a small plastic tube she inhales enough to move the world around. Finally, she gathers the remains scattered over the surface with the tip of one of her fingers and rubs her gums with it.

Title holder of the stars, she changes their course at will, to have them in her favour. In the meantime, on the TV screen, an abstract zapping rambles through her eyes.

The topaz of twilight lies behind the horizon and the stars take hold in the sky. It has been a while since the neon lights last kissed Alicia. With tablets, she wakes the mornings up. And sleeping pills dry the nights. Cocaine to lift up, alcohol to soften up. Besides, if the mirror does not show her what she wants, in the bathroom cabinet a dose of cyanide awaits its turn; but it´s time to go.

The lipstick struggles against Alicia´s lips, and covers the contours of flesh that won't smile. The course of her eyelids, a naked line of mascara, where weariness strolls. Onyx cuticles with glamour nail polish. Thread of nausea that won´t confess.

With close-fitting fashion clothes, Alicia emphasizes her curves. She knows what appeals the most about her wardrobe and she uses it. Last but not least, she hides her female smell behind an imported fragrance.

She builds a remix version of her character to relate to others[2]. Honesty burns her lips, but lying is sweet. The mirror shows a bad replica of herself, still it works. This way, other people´s neurosis doesn´t hurt, as she moves around unregistered in a staged city.

The night, starry panther, finds her limit on a fragile transverse line proposed by the sea. Hidden by the dun silence, the sounds of cars reverberate. The salt seasoned breeze polishes people´s faces, as they look at the silver refection left by the moon on the water´s liquid anarchy.

Over plastic streets, Velcro parks and spongy neoprene buildings grow. An invisible phosphorescence, almost indifferent, surrounds them. On her way to work, Alicia can see, through her car´s windshield, how

---

[2] Personality is a piece of paper that folds in to conceal different sides and display others, like an Origami.

the trees project their branches on the tunnel they form along the street, as well as the street signs and lights. With a slight turn of her head, she can get a better look at how traffic intertwines, other driver´s faces, a pedestrian in the distance.

Beside the sweet asphalt, traffic lights are outlaws, free zones where red lights stop no one. Inside Alicia´s car, images happen faster than God. Speed in the peace of those who are on the verge of suicide, she accelerates the cylinder of the Russian Roulette, where bets run like adrenalin tokens. Past the avenue, her foot releases its tension on the gas pedal and, with a relief of the engine, Alicia decides that the show is over. She makes a right at the first gas station, and continues, with a calm pace, to do the last few yards until the inertia of routine forces her to stop. She sets herself free from her synthetic coated metal cage, and breathes in the fresh air from the outside. Under the trees, her footsteps follow the rows of concrete tile which end at an old door. And, once again, it is the same wood that sounds when she knocks.

Facing the old door, he adjusts the silk tie he bought in the morning, along with the straight dark woolen suit he is wearing. He turns his left sleeve and checks the time in his watch. Since the arm is already up, he takes his palm to his mouth and exhales in it to test if his breath still smells like mint. For the last time, he verifies that everything is where it is supposed to be and, before ringing the doorbell, he smells the flowers he is holding in his right hand. The buzz doesn´t keep him waiting. He pushes the door with the tip of his fingers and enters a yellow walled hall that grows into a stairway with wooden handrails on both sides. His feet, wedged into shiny black shoes, step on every other white granite tread, reaching the top. A receptionist in a long garment and expensive hairstyle awaits.

As he completes the tour to the first floor, he remembers how, every Thursday, at the same time, for the past year, from behind the thick blue velvet drapery that separates the room adjacent to the stairs, Alicia appears as a prototype of purity. Dressed in a tiny lingerie outfit, see-through nightgown and matching high heel shoes, a different hairstyle every time. With only one shift, every word weighs. Thus, he can recall how they both say «I missed you", "I love you", " I like you very much", "so do I". The night would be timeless if it wasn't for that damn fist knocking at the door, relentlessly marking the end of the visit.

Upstairs, invariably, the likeable receptionist greets him with a kiss. However, with her particular sweetness, she informs him that this time Alicia is busy, and she will see him in a few minutes. Without losing composure, he notices that a slight nervous tic in his right eyebrow makes him uncomfortable. In spite of this, he insists in asking the very well attired woman if maybe Alicia is not yet dressed, to which she warmly answers "no, at this moment she is with another client, and as soon as she is available he will be able to see his lover". He stands still for a moment to finally lose himself with his flowers in the staircase. The bang at the door is the last thing heard from him.

Homemade food has, among its characteristics, the fondness and high quality of its ingredients. Under this concept, one might say that eating at a restaurant would be culinary prostitution, and you wouldn´t be wrong. The same concept does not apply to paid sex hunger, and those who are accustomed to this service don´t make any carnal fast vows. When the algorithms of desire hit harder than usual, they know the sweet wooden scent of females from their own species anaesthetizes them. Refinement keeps us apart from animals, but not from our instincts, heartbeats that are prior to our bodies.

In the classified ad section of one of the local newspapers, right before the Judicial Edicts, there are headings such as "masseuse" or "services", where Jennifer, Pamela and Barbie, provoke the most sophisticated perversions. Women with exceptional bodies, owners of excellent virtues, but with incredibly long phone numbers.

At the private house, buzzes go on and off, and the men of desire parade. With their bills they bring life to the place, along with McDonald´s smiles and the sensual manners of the prostitutes.

Alicia lives in a city where fake money and disappointments abound. The financial crisis brings about frigidity, and this increases the genital hire, a situation which she takes advantage of, absorbing cash from helpless penises, and harvesting bison´s affection, frog´s love, boar´s passion, hen´s petting and donkey´s understanding. Still, there are times when work becomes a party: two clients at a time, sometimes three. Hopefully, a client requests two ladies and the craft really becomes pleasure.

Thus, condom after condom, from dusk till dawn, her industry grows along with her vocation for service.

Rumor has it there is a bum in town who walks down to the beach at sunrise to show his ass to the Sun. Alicia would be glad to do that too, but after work other activities are on schedule. If desire was her religion, surely her body would be her temple. Firm flesh has stock market value, therefore she is the first one to show up at the gym on the corner, to tone up her muscles and reduce the excess body weight. Tanning bed, change in hair style, nail work, all call for her; and they all have a price. Making this doll factory affordable is reason enough for Alicia to report to work every day.

The beautification session is over, and for Alicia it is another day in the office. She doesn't appeal to memory to compare today to yesterday, she just does her job and leaves. By the sidewalk, her car engine is infected with laziness, responding hoarsely to the touch. The exhaust pipe releases thick puffs of smoke, which bounce and expand in slow motion against the street. Covered in dew, the windshield filters the colors of the morning.

In Alicia, the night shift produces an anonymous hangover which turns driving into an involuntary act. The metallic morning traffic tide is denser than usual. Inside the disturbing enclosure of her car, reflections without shadows of a thousand blades hit the lady, eager to finish her trip once and for all. On the radio, a catchy song which she used to sing in another time now becomes unbearable. Moisture lost in the high tide that falls on the brand new blouse. Outside the window, a driver speeds up his car, another one honks, a third one swears; you know, street courtesy. Before her eyes, the usual images return. In the bus stop, an *Arcor* advertising sign is the backstage. The digits of a *Casio* watch show 10:35. A yellow *Mercedez Benz* bus with a *Disco* ad stops in front of her. While she waits, people with *Le Uthe* shirts, *Dufour* pants, *Hush Puppies* shoes, *Midway* jackets and *Route 66* sweatshirts parade along the sidewalk. She resumes her movement, but is soon distracted by the pictures around her: *Simplesse* signs, *Ford's* new model on a poster, *Coca-Cola* neon signs, *IBM* ads. The *Nivea* billboard indicates the end of the journey. She parks her car, and starts walking along the concrete carpet, cold waterproof granite tiles which isolate her from the crude nature, up to the entrance of the building where she is staying. Inside, the publicity disappears for a moment and pastel color walls, stainless steel elevators, and fake wood siding panels appear. But it comes back when she turns on the TV, like a robot, after entering her apartment. Underneath the door, a few letters stick out; they may very well be from that container for unwanted relationships, the family; or from the Guinness Book, to let her know she holds the loneliness record. But no. Just a few useless brochures, and tax bills, which the direct debit will pay.

She was waited for all night by someone, her pet. A beautiful "tea with cream" fur ball, who receives her at the door jumping and barking, and won´t let her advance towards the answering machine which, by the way, hasn't given away a single message in a long time. Thankfully, the appliances show some faithfulness, and they make the hours before bed tolerable. If the Electricity Company doesn't decide to shut off the energy supply, these close friends, with an automatic and inorganic conscience, will help her zip her soul shut.

In the bedroom, a furniture piece is happy to see her. Her sheets are still messed up and they have been calling for her body since the previous afternoon. To one side, on the bedside table, the blow smiles. Insolent mineral, if Alicia doesn't make it in the morning, without coming back to that contact, she becomes naked by the shadows left by its absence. Demon who won't run away from God, that son of a bitch doesn't know mercy.

Her day is about to end. The five senses flee, her molars tighten against each other, her features tense, even her thoughts harden. Having lost consciousness, she dreams a mummies' dream.

In the meantime, on the TV screen, an abstract zapping rambles through her eyes again.

Alicia has been less willing to wait lately; so, when she comes into the room, the gentleman who has been expecting her for intimate pleasures, is already in bed, naked and displaying a satisfaction smile. He hopes for that figure, fit in a tight black leather corset, high heel boots in the same color, fishnet stockings, hair tied back with a metallic buckle, eyebrows trimmed and lined, lips of an incandescent red, the visible parts of her body painted white, and four sets of handcuffs in one of her hands. He is very specific about the service he wants and, if Alicia doesn't mind, she sometimes assumes different roles according to the client's preferences. All this, of course, at a higher price than usual.

Sometimes she wears a mask, sometimes she doesn't. He is curious about what makes her decide each time, but he doesn't dare to ask her. She gets close, and while she kisses him, she handcuffs his extremities to the bed frame. He does not show the slightest resistance. It doesn't take long before the hands and feet go blue from the strangulation, but he doesn't complain. Then, she sits on his crotch, and rubs her body against his in a continuous back and forth movement. After a while, Alicia notices he hasn't been stimulated enough and, smiling, she reprimands him: "You are a pervert!" Next, she opens the bedside table drawer, and takes out a transparent plastic bag, with which she wraps his bold head and clean-shaven face, to finally tie it strongly around his neck. The air that he breathes, captured inside the bag, makes the plastic contract and expand around the customer's face. Alicia can feel how his organ begins to harden, hard enough to fit the condom. After that, she takes off her thong, introduces his member and starts to move again, this time she goes up and down.

From inside the steamy bag, he screams: "Choke me! Choke me!"

Alicia wraps his neck with both hands, and tightly squeezes his throat. After a few moans, the gentleman ejaculates. Immediately, Alicia releases the pressure on the throat, and unties the plastic bag, which results in an endless inhalation by the suffocated body. She gets up, removes the handcuff from one of his hands, and throws the keys on his face. Before she leaves she yells: "You better not take so long next time!"

With its back to the shore, the sky fleshes out on the great wall of buildings. Over the misaligned horizon of the terraces, a sea of antennas germinates. The birds, once they have crossed that abyss where their arms stretch, abuse those metallic branches, unaware of the images they collect. They watch the granite and concrete streets where Alicia walks, as she hopes the shop windows will distract her. A path inhabited by "no news" looks, indifferent lips, bidet hearts, anonymous mediocrity.

In her gestures, apart from the miseries, in the hallways, under the sky, amongst the bricks, every time she combs her hair, through the windows, when greeting somebody, when she blinks, in the morning, in the empty spaces between street signs, around the corners, when she pays with fives, on park benches, repeated in every chord, in her pockets, when she feels the night, even if she hasn't been faithful to September, even after waking up crippled, even if she rests in a coma and the auroras are others, Alicia calmly begins to hate her job.

That healthy resentment against males turns the unenthusiastic penetrations of the day tolerable. Docile currency, sprouting within a fire that won't recede, no matter how much jewelry invades her trenches. All these emotions crash against the old wooden door, where her shift awaits. The metallic push button cedes easily to the finger pressure and, almost instantly, the buzz indicates the beginning of the new turn.

In the afternoon the hallway becomes darker and there is a smell of surgery room, which is forgotten at the top of the stairs. Then, Alicia enters the kitchen, where she greets her co-workers, who are expecting their next clients in her sexy garments. After that, she heads into the ladies room to change. In her bag, she carries everything she needs. She takes her sneakers, jeans, and t-shirt off, and puts on fancy lingerie and high heel shoes.

It doesn't take long before the first applicant shows up. He is usually required to wait a few minutes in a room with a dim light and comfortable sofas, adjacent to the blue velvet curtain hall. However, as frequent as their visits may be, and although they pretend to be at ease, there is always a tension before entering the bedrooms, especially if there are other men, like them, waiting.

When the time is right, the customer enters one of the rooms and, without delay, those girls who are available go in, one by one, they greet the men with a kiss, introduce themselves with their fantasy name, turn around and leave. When the round is finished, the receptionist informs the client about the different services and rates. He confesses his wish, who he wants it fulfilled with, and pays. After collecting the money, the lady in charge asks him to make himself comfortable and heads towards the kitchen where she meets the girls. She informs the chosen one about the service requested and the rate agreed on. Next, they fill out a form, where they include all the transaction details, as well as the date and time of the deal. Last, the signature. At the end of the day, the subtotals are added up and divided by two, half for the house and the rest for the worker. The cost of classified ads and security is also discounted.

After a month's combat, anyone is a veteran. The ladies adjust the tone of her voices from person to person. They handle latex like chewing gum, placing it with their mouths without the patron even noticing.

As their lips suck the warm, laminated object, they think about the new purse they'll be able to buy, or those shoes that are in style these days, so high but now affordable; or about expensive parties and even about renting their own apartment. The meticulous oral elevator job gradually catches a rhythm and, the more they wander, the more enthusiastic the sucking gets. They no longer care about the adhesive taste of the condom of choice, or about the emery hands stroking their foam sculpted hair. When they feel they are slightly "wet" by these games, a little saliva at the Venus Gate will facilitate the penetration. Surprised, men usually come beforehand and, absorbed by their fire, the ladies fail to perceive it. They never imagined this job could be so easy, they consider the ejaculations the measure of their wealth. Still, they are exhausted, after twenty four hours of hormonal swinging.

From time to time, if there are people waiting, they are kindly asked by the receptionist to lock themselves up inside a room. Not a very frequent situation, this is sometimes requested by some important public figures, who value their privacy very much. Within the silence of the room, the confined can hear the footsteps from the other side of the wall. Their confused eyes turn to one another and they wander: Who could it be? A politician? An entrepreneur? A priest? A judge? How much is he paying? Double? Triple?

Their arrival is always welcomed by the women in the house, even though they are generally pretentious and demanding. In the kitchen, the ladies anxiously await the arrival of the receptionist. After a few minutes, the door opens and the woman in charge names the winner of the first prize: Alicia. She is sitting in a corner, applying varnish on her nails and, with an imperceptible face gesture, she gets up to put her signature on the form.

When entering the room, the character's silhouette does not give her the best impression, but it is her job, and sometimes she doesn't get to choose. She tries to relax and confidently asks the client some personal questions. Seduced, the man answers gladly, shortening the distance between them. Alicia's hands stroke his chest, softly run through his shoulders, and then unbutton his jacket. Next, she holds the lapels and pushes them backwards, allowing the jacket to slide down his back and off his arms. Later, she caresses his neck and neatly loosens up his tie. Now she unbuttons his shirt revealing the greyish commander's chest. She feels the belt buckle under his belly and, in a few blind maneuvers she unfastens it, showing the zipper on his outdated trousers. Using one of her hands, she unzips him and pulls out his member, which is already hardened. Alicia judges it is time to reach for the condom, always available on the bedside table. Her teeth open the plastic wrapping and pull out the latex ring, which she then places over the tip of his cannon. She pulls it down to unroll it but it doesn't happen. She realizes she put it on backwards. He gives a nasty look at her. She turns it over and now she slides it down easily. Kneeling before her opponent, she stares at his straight member, very close to her mouth, and remembers the lessons she received from a colleague who usually carries that thick and voluminous book full of metaphors, the I Ching, to play with coins. Among its proverbs, she read that "inferior dominates superior" and, "from underneath it imposes itself". In a different situation she would have pleased the guy with her carnal skills. But today, she wanders why she is being subdued, considering she loathes that flesh and skin pole, the cornerstone that makes men what they are. Alicia's hate is released through the man's raw scream as she pulls her sharp teeth away from his organ.

And with that cry, out go the hair salons, the manicures, the expensive lingerie, the gym, and tanning beds. Except for those consequences, she experiences a strange combination of weariness and dignity[3].

---

[3] There are some undesirable doors which we are forced to cross,

boredom sieves which talismans can't free you from. Those bars mist up the dusks sowing the wires of doubt. That which is fleeting causes pain.

Bars aren't what they used to be. Sitting somewhere, Alicia can't find on the menu the one thing she is interested in. Bereft of company, she finishes her coffee without paying attention to it. In the cup's bottom, the coffee dregs don't predict any luck. A cigarette that ceased to be abandons its ash vestige inside a bowl showing an aperitif ad. Her reflection on the glass cuts out her loneliness' silhouette. Humidity is a translucent mesh where images are filtered. Cars pass by, people walk, trees are moved by the wind, birds caw, anything but a song, the TV with its stupidity, everything conspires. In her mind, the films of the past roll, but she prefers to amuse herself with media heroes and encoded gods from the screen. Finally, a gesture from the cashier relieves her anxiety, as she hastily walks towards the restrooms. Behind her, the employee walks in and, after closing the door, he checks out the place. In this sanitary privacy, face to face, each one delivers the expected good, to receive the desired one "": A small sack wrapped around itself many times separates the blow from the buyers' touch. Without tearing the insulation, she unties the knot and pours the contents on top of her fist. Alicia in the sky with diamonds, she bites the crystals that transform her into a deity. She feeds her nose, hoping to extinguish the suffering. If it depended on her, this moment would be her eternity, but the future becomes the past before turning into the present.

Back at the table, she washes down with alcohol what cocaine lifts up, a chemical roller-coaster heading towards a dark fire, worse than any torture. Deep down, there's neither time nor love. A miserable never-ending lethargy that shadows don't take pity on.

Slave to Alicia's petting, her dog awaits her on the worn-out sidewalk adjacent to the bar, attentive to every movement coming from the door. After a long wait, the pet gets its reward and receives it with joy. Alicia, even in this elation, caresses its long blond hair and feels the need for a cigarette, but she only has a few threads of tobacco left on the base of the wrinkled package. A few feet away, a kiosk pacifies her restlessness. She searches the bottom of her purse for the last coins and she buys a pack with them. The cellophane easily gives its impenetrability between Alicia's nails. A light cylinder breaks out of the package and makes it to her fleshy rouge lips. The metallic paper, the aroma of fresh tobacco, and the taste of the first smoke share the exaltation. In her handbag yesterday weighs more than usual. As she resumes the path, the next puffs speak to her about unreachable worlds and infinite gods, but her instinct tells her that it is time to go back. Nostalgia irrigates her steps, while the sun dries her footprints. With an empty wallet, Alicia is dragged to the urban latrine, where the tiny sack of recently purchased hydrochloride becomes money again.

Thus, she comes full circle; the B side of society coexists intertwined and invisible and, like a dog that learns how to hurt himself, all that matters is how to get high and what stops you from doing it. She doesn't need Nostradamus to know that it'll all go to hell. Human kind might as well blow out altogether, so it won't have to be put up with any longer.

""The need is constant, but the money is scarce. However, the Bag Man (Boogie Man) is a good person and takes good care of us. Santa Claus with snow in a sack deals the cards .Those who come to him want something for their heads and, one by one, they leave satisfied. Everyone's "Foot" and it's everyone's hand, nobody calls "Bluff". He delivers ten and they yield seven, the best way extremities know how to clean each other.

Entangled in the wind's music, with no rhyme; the trees, undernourished by winter, hide their secrets from goblins, bills made of bone that the morning dries. Down rivers that fail to flow into the ocean, Miss Eclipse salts the honey from disesteemed days. Except for her clothes, her black hair roots, her face with no makeup on, the sun tan slipping from her body, nails trying to restore their natural color, the bus trips, the simpler meals, a telephone that doesn't work, and living in a cheap motel, for her, everything is still in its place.

The light of day comes slower every time. The slabs from buildings mutilate the sky in its background. Touch overlaps sensations, although it is the senses that present the real obstacles. She knows that it is a breeze what she feels, as she continues her steps delayed by the street sounds.

The soul's cavities keep her awake, worthy of her anorexic feelings, hanging from the wall of shame with hypocrisy pins. Life, in the verge of men, is a long-awaited hell.

Her need changes with the city. Under a salt disguise, alien to her own feelings, she seeks refuge in movie theaters, black boxes where she reclaims spare mornings. In the meantime, with her shadow, she longs to be a simple occupant of borrowed stories.

Displaced from the social sketch, she observes her unfinished silhouette rambling on a curtain made of irregular tiles. She doesn't want to go through the main arteries, but rather drink the sap from unsigned streets, and apologize to pedestrians for not having gods to respond to. In the kingdom of internet and omission, truth is the number one public enemy. Although she bites the bread of forgiveness, that so called "conscious reality" scares her like an epidemic. Imprecision is a life-long river.

For someone who has been awake for several days, the break of dawn happens in slow motion4. For Alicia, the best way to skip it is to find one of those places where she can stay if necessary. She has been choosing to eat all kinds of grass lately, and she comes to this neighborhood where poverty looks better, when the weak and distant lamps light up the night. She visits the place that the habitués call "The Needle House". Cornered by a hamlet of metal sheet shacks, the house is the vestige of long gone prosperity. Although the deterioration of the walls and the shattered window panes are visible, time and apathy have not been able to conceal its magnificence. In it reside a polite drug dealer (with several bodyguards) who, like a good host, allows his customers to spend the night when they pass out.

In one of the bedrooms, a group of strangers rest on a few sofas or on the carpeted floor. Alicia sits in a corner on the floor with her back against the wall. On a coffee table, to

---

4 Time goes by as long as it has space to do so. The hours used to leave behind a scent, but lately they melt leaving no tracks in the memory. A never-ending present after present folded in its extremes.

one side, the instruments of her disgrace rest: a spoon carbonized by use, a pile of match boxes, a pack of cotton, a bottle of mineral water, a rubber band and a recently used syringe.

In order to rinse out the interior, Alicia introduces the needle in the water, she fills the tube completely and expels the content. Then she checks the miserable bounty she has recently purchased to later pour, with shaky hands, a little cocaine in the spoon and adds some water. Next, she lights up an entire box of matches and, using it as a burner, she heats up the solution until all the crystals are dissolved. She then places a piece of cotton inside the spoon in order to get it soaked in the warm liquid. Using the cotton as a filter, Alicia sticks the needle tip on the cotton ball and sucks the content in until only air bubbles enter the pipe. After that, she aims for the roof with the syringe and squeezes it until the first stream comes out, evidence that no more air is in the tube, only the translucent fluid.

With the loaded and ready to fire gun on the table, Alicia looks for her target. For every scalpel that is born, there is one body demanding the taste of its blade. She strips her right arm, with the rubber band she prepares a tourniquet around the biceps, and she scans the inner face of her arm for a spot where the itinerary of a vein hasn't been intercepted by the tip of a needle. She notices this is a difficult task, but she finally finds a minuscule space near the mark left by the last pinch. She drives the needle into that spot, but, instead of injecting the content, she absorbs some blood and waits for an instant to allow the fluids to blend.

Now the solution is ready, she puts pressure on the cylinder and travels to her dream of omnipotence. But this time, the hydrochloride boomerang hits harder than ever. In her mind, her brother's words boom: "Never through the veins! You hear me!, Ever!".

Suspended images, film squares stop abruptly as time becomes flaccid, impotent for action. Memory stays in a room apart. She, without herself, connected to the world by a thin consciousness. Too much anxiety suffocates her, and everything moves her.

Images take place faster than God. The fate of consciousness abandons her as she falls into a dark nightmare. Figures of twilight that change in a footless puzzle. Time returns to a lethargic chaos, almost impossible to remember, with incoherent shapes and disconnected phrases. Centuries filtered of images that, like far away waters, fall down without disappointment.

In the midst of this confusion, a dream arises. Alicia faces the darkness, where she can hardly appreciate the outline of things around her. Not knowing exactly what, she searches within the flooding milkiness that impedes her movement. Uncertainty exasperates her.

A shadow bursts in the scene, provoking nauseating hate and revenge sensations in her. A hunt unfolds instincts without truce, inside lanes that she can barely see; a flabby labyrinth, vaguely limited, where the shadow clumsily breaks out from Alicia's chase. Until it hits a wall, inside a blind alley. Cornered and exhausted, the shadow gives in to its enemy who, at a short distance, stops in her tracks and stares at it. With mallets and blades Alicia opens her victim's chest and eats up its bowels. At that moment, the milky darkness that surrounds them diminishes. Before them, a mirror appears reflecting the victim, and Alicia recognizes in it that her lunch is no one but herself. In the horror caused by this vision, Alicia releases a heartbreaking scream that wakes her up.

An indefinite load of pain nests on Alicia's face. The sounds, images, and smells of the room reappear, almost translucent. Within a deaf rumor, reaching from one corner of the room, she recognizes random words. They are an addict's words who, in his delirium, moves his hands around and mumbles incomprehensible sentences. Everyone in the room is almost frozen, scattered around the floor; except for one, oddly obese, who clumsily crawls towards Alicia, as she incubates her narcolepsy, sweating cold, and shivering hot.

Inside the incongruous monologue, Alicia manages to distinguish a slight buzz. It seems distant at first but, in time, she gets to localize it near her. Because of the contrast with her skin she recognizes the blurry outline of a mosquito that maneuvers around her and, after a few failed attempts, lands on her arm. With its wings still, she observes in detail how it searches for a spot on her surface and, also, how its sting demands the fluid inside her. Little by little the insect's abdomen swells, turning its dark color into bright crimson. Without her noticing, the mosquito disappears, crushed by a big, heavy hand. Alicia feels the thump in the distance and contemplates how the owner of that hand brings it close to his round and baggy eyed face, to later lick the remains of the crushed insect. The tone of his veined skin is highlighted underneath his extra-large worn out clothes.

For a while, the pale sumo wrestler dully smells her, enjoying, and then lays his body by her side. Once in a convenient position, he directs his head towards the motionless lady's neck and opens his jaws to display some oversize fangs which he uses to pierce her flesh without delay. She feels how her body's fluids reduce, powerless to stop it. An instant later, the huge addict rolls away on his back next to Alicia, his lips stained with her liquid, and passes out leaving his victim with half her blood.

After the trance, she has a headache which is impossible to localize, and holes on her neck. Her hands are numb, almost insensitive, but slowly they begin to respond to her orders, now with greater strength. She notices that her arms, as well as the rest of her body, have that tone. Her sharp senses find smells never perceived before, touch without pain, taste without palate, vision without imagination, memory without feelings. Inside this universe eager to be discovered, she understands with fresh cleverness that the sumo fighter did more than just suck her blood; he also injected his own killer thirst into her.

Outside the house, her pet waits for her to come out, but this time, its wagging tail slows down as Alicia walks towards it, until it stops. Its ears withdraw, its hackles rise, its lips tense up, letting its deep growl be heard from within its fangs. And that is the last image they shared.

The sun reads faces; that's why, at night, there are places where Alicia finds affinities[5]. They are "desire pals" who get together to buy and consume substances. But these are always scant, so the pinball of circumstances drives them to pizzerias or restaurants owned by some acquaintance, who sells to be able to consume, without having his budget altered. Or third rate night clubs, where they buy cheap, even if quality is not guaranteed. And tonight is not a lucky night. Alicia saves for herself a little blow which is not enough to share with her friends, and they decide to head to this new place, where they know of a point man they can meet.

---

[5] Whether it is because they share the same tastes or for chemical kinship, consuming the same substances makes them family.

Before the entrance, at each side of the door, two men stand, they are more skilled to hit than to work. Inside, shadows trimmed from the smoke are intercepted by the sounds in their non-stop cadence. Alicia dances, when an occasional presence appeals to her. A dark silhouette with its long skirt, traces an inverted flame movement as it marches: It is a serene looking maiden, like clean silk who, without slowing her pace, sets her eyes on Alicia, and uncovers a face which is the most delicate among all the tones of white possible. Freshness that invites with a smile on iridescent lips. An instant look that reveals Alicia's heaven. In the damsel's heart, the beats of an unstoppable feeling burst. With no answer, she follows Alicia's steps. In her mind, the briefness of that expression shuts her feelings off. Without giving herself permission, she discovers worship.

Little by little, their looks come closer and they share their movements. Everything is alright for Alicia, the addictive sisterhood is obvious, an extra motivation that invites her.

The night prospers, with the thirst for sensations that walk with the young friends.

Distant from any place, near the rhythm, the resonant contortions go together with the House fever. Alicia finds approval in someone else's eyes, meridian of an early femininity.

Far from being unnoticed, these unprecedented fleshes call for hawks: Lesbians, like vaginal males in heat, circle around the delicacy. Their agitated udders anticipate pleasures with a body that is sexually unknown. Alicia enjoys the scene without interfering. She wouldn't want the spell to fade, together with the artificial smoke, and the acid semi gods surrounding her. This odd peacock procession decorates the set, adding color to her self-esteem.

The Extra Brut goes around, and the maiden gives in to the temptation of its delicate bubbles. The fizziness on her nose provides a fun touch to the smooth taste. Without a satellite signal to guide her, the joy begins, together with the dizziness. In the meantime, Alicia repays with smiles and an innocent kiss on the cheek, followed by other kisses. Hands caress one another, arms intertwine, as breasts hold tightly. Lips that search through cheeks, until they find their species' concern.

Leaving the dance floor, heading to the restrooms, they go around moving obstacles through this soggy maze. Opening the door to the only lit room in the place, the blinding light hits them; they go in all the same. In the crowded place the ladies smoke, put their make up on, or chat with some guy.

A toilet becomes available and the young friends take the opportunity to lock themselves in. There is more philosophy than insult in lavatory graffiti. Alicia opens her purse and takes out a pack of maxi pads, she searches the bottom and finds a small bag. Using one nail, she extracts from the inside a tiny portion of the white and obedient powder, which she cunningly brings closer to her nose, and inhales. She repeats the procedure and offers a pinch to her friend. The snow penetrates like an inverted waterfall until it disappears. They linger in their sanitary universe as the miracle happens. They look into the heat of a feeling they cannot reject. This event surprises them but in no way scares them. Artificial courage keeps them warm, where no obstacle is impossible to challenge. It is hard to remember whose initiative it was, but they perceive the noble wood scent coming from the other body. With burning fingertips, their hands become time. Alicia brands affection tattoos on the maiden's porcelain surface. Touch that travels through uncountable shapes. Deep and outlined track, where her name penetrates, to stop at that place where texture changes: toy nipples on firm breasts that respond without shivering, as lips converse in mute contact. Games are gradually diverted towards less decent zones. Alicia follows the root of instinct and the brushes maneuver south of the abdomen where, underneath layers of delicate fabric, the lady conceals warm hairs. The fairy holds a grip on moist flesh, subterranean and alive. Their desperate fingers seek sepulcher in that depression. Animal groove that civilization hasn't been able to subdue. Virility that bursts in a hormonal storm. Profane ecstasy, worth living and repeating. The damsel, giving her consent without objection, tones her laughter down into a soft moan. Their lips touch other, more frail, lips, and rub silky skin on soft bones. Her body breathes with forced cadence as fingers explore more sensitive areas. A rapture cloud wraps them. A glass is shattered and is heard in another galaxy.

Alicia's teeth bite nipples one more time and they head south, to the hollow space where everything is possible. The bee encircles the flower. The petals, excited by the buzzing sound, open wide. The insect dives in, holds its tongue, penetrating scarlet passages, including the most intimate pulp, and drinks unmentionable fluids.

The sublime moment approaches. Without missing the pace, Alicia holds her laborious kiss, to continue with her fingertips again. The fairy stands up slowly, making sure her friend doesn't lose her arousal. From this geography everything flows smoothly. Her look, portrayal of the fairy, runs through corporeal shades sculpted by genes and mysteries, as she parks the image on a neatly polished shoulder. When the climax is imminent, Alicia sinks some powerful fangs on her neck and sucks. What matters is not the blood itself, only what it carries. Her taste, now more refined than ever, can detect the hemoglobin, the alcohol, the nicotine, but also the testosterone and the dopamine. However, she cannot resist the taste of hydrochloride. She knows that by drinking it, the speed and intensity of the effect are less than when sniffed or injected, but it is so addictive, that she draws out all the blood from her friend until she empties her completely. Then, she wipes the remaining blood off from her lips with her sleeves and feels like drawing on the steamy mirrors in front of her with it, but she remembers that they will never again return her reflection back to her.

Coming out of the restroom, she meets again the crowd in the stroboscopic darkness, the unbearable decibels, the sluggish air. Tired and wearing a headache, Alicia realizes that although she is half dead, this really *is* living. She decides to leave, before the sun hits her sensitive body. She takes a few steps on the sidewalk, the dew of sunrise awaits her, but she runs away, in complicity with the silence that she wraps up as she stomps along.

The apartment where Alicia used to live with her pet and her nightmares has had a new tenant for several months. In the bedroom, a huge bulk tries to get out of bed. Despite her massive body, she moves with lightness, turns on the light and takes a deep breath in order to contemplate the situation: a lamp with a white shade embroidered in color, dimly lights the pastel painted walls of the room, its windows shut. The informal design furniture contains textbooks that are still in use, as well as a collection of teddy bears and dolls. On the wall, a poster of a passionate Freddy Mercury is the center of attention. A quilt and matching color cushions cover the bed, on which Alicia laughs at everything. On the floor, by her side lies the cold body of that who was just a moment ago, the occupant of the place.

It's close to eight p.m. and it's hunting time. Alicia verifies that the sun is really hidden and only then, she leaves the apartment; maneuvering to pass through the door opening. Without turning on the hallway lights, she heads to the elevator and pushes the button. With a brisk noise, the elevator lets her know it has stopped and, as she opens the door, a passenger inside cannot hide his surprise. Underneath a black tunic, a two hundred kilogram body displays only the head, thick pale arms rutted by blue veins, a round and puffy-eyed face, and messy hair.

Alicia smells her fellow traveller, but she does not detect anything appealing. It's been a while since the hemoglobin stopped being a priority for her, and she searches through darker places, for what really feeds her. The trip ends with another crude noise in the lobby and Alicia comes out of the elevator without looking back at her companion who, from the inside, still hesitates to get out.

Once in the street, she lifts her head up and sniffs a couple of times, but she does not perceive in the air a victim's scent. It is time to move towards places that offer more possibilities. She stops a cab and the very first puff of air inside the car tells her that the driver is a consumer. She takes a seat and gives him a vague destination. The vehicle starts and heads towards the avenue. The traffic is heavy, but it does not stop Alicia from sinking her fangs into the driver's neck. He picks his hands up from the wheel and, even though he struggles as hard as he can, he cannot break free from her. The steering wheel, completely loose, can't make up its mind which way to go. It doesn't matter anymore, the car deviates from the road, causing a multiple crash. The taxi's interior becomes a blender, in which the occupants bounce against each other, the walls, the windows and the plastic coverings. Several volunteers approach to help Alicia out of the wrecked car. After many attempts, they manage to get her out, dragging her away from the pile of twisted metal. Absent from all the commotion, she stands up, she straightens up her broken bones, which immediately weld themselves together, and she wipes off the blood from her already healed wounds. Then, she walks away before the amazed witnesses.

With her clothes torn and her make-up running down from her face, Alicia makes it to the syringe house. The owner, after the first shock, recognizes her voice and becomes happy to see her. It's been two hundred kilos since she was here for the last time, when she came, apathetic, with her dog. Everything inside looks the same, but it is the penetrating smell of warm bodies loaded with hydrochloride which thrills her.

The owner, the only one to greet her, becomes the first victim. After that, she continues with those scattered all over the living room sofas and then, those in the bedrooms. There is only one left in the bathroom who, after he is done, opens the door to find Alicia's face, soaked in blood. She lashes out against him and absorbs his fluid all the way to the last drop. Exhausted, she gives in next to the withered body and falls asleep.

Through the faceted skylight, the first ray of sun penetrates and lights up the bathroom interior. The light coming from the medicine cabinet adds up. With his pants down, the dried up corpse of the last victim lies on the floor. Unwilling to wake him up, to one side, rest the ashes accumulated after the combustion of that who was, just a moment ago, the Blood's Daughter[6].

---

[6] Oblivion is the right of those who are absent. Death, a common territory.